For Rosa
and her fairy godmother,
Naomi

First published 1997 by Walker Books Ltd
87 Vauxhall Walk, London SE11 5HJ

This edition published 2008

10 9 8 7 6 5 4 3 2 1

© 1997 Bob Graham

The moral rights of the author-illustrator
have been asserted.

This book has been typeset
in Garamond Book Educational.

Printed in China

British Library Cataloguing in Publication Data:
a catalogue record for this book
is available from the British Library.

ISBN 978-1-4063-1648-3

www.walkerbooks.co.uk

Queenie
the
Bantam

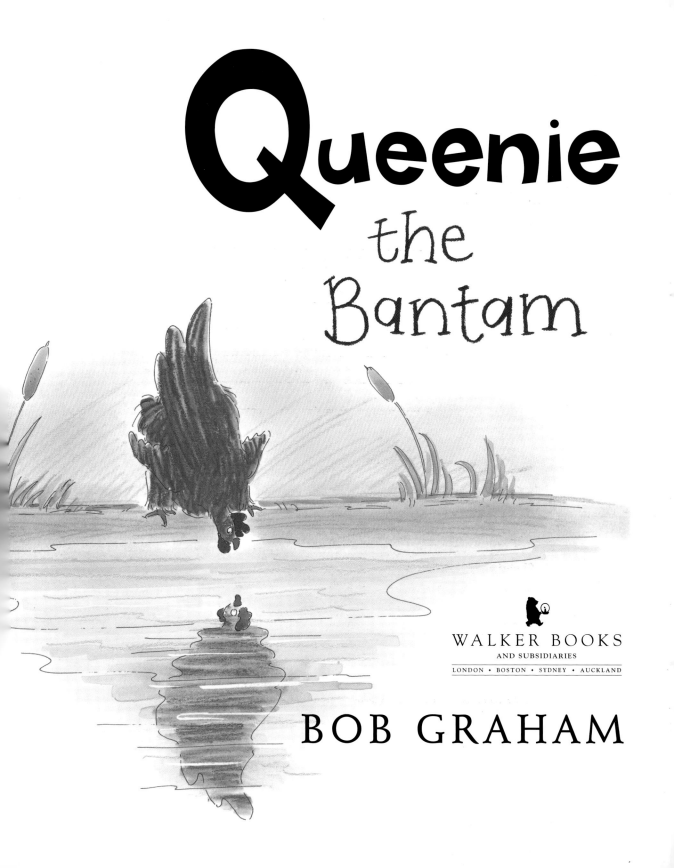

WALKER BOOKS
AND SUBSIDIARIES
LONDON • BOSTON • SYDNEY • AUCKLAND

BOB GRAHAM

"**Look!**" said Caitlin's dad.
"What is it?" asked Caitlin's mum.
"It's a hen in the lake,"
   replied Dad, and he
   did not hesitate.

Off came his shoes, off came his socks,

off came his hat, off came Caitlin!

Caitlin's dad knew that the hen was in trouble.
Big trouble!

"She's a bantam,"
said Mum.

"Wrap her up warm,"
said Dad.

"What's your name, then? Hatty? Tessa? Molly?"
said Mum. "No, Queenie! I think
you're a Queenie!"

That might have been
the end of the story … but it wasn't!

Queenie was soon
very much at home
in Bruno's basket.

And, in time, Queenie saw
Caitlin's first steps –
   one,
     two,
       three.
Queenie had become one
of the family.

But Caitlin's mum knew
that Queenie had
a home of
her own.

"I think she lives on the farm over the hill from the lake,"
said Mum. So Mum and Dad and Caitlin
and Bruno set off for the farm.

Mum was right.
This was Queenie's home.

Caitlin, her mum and dad
and Bruno the dog came
home with milk and cheese
and fresh eggs.

And Bruno got his
basket back.

That might have been
the end of the story …
but it wasn't!

The next morning,
Queenie got up before the sun.

She flew over the fence, ran along the path and
past the churchyard.

She went around the lake

and through the woods …

over the road,

across the park …

and down the street to Caitlin's house.

And in Bruno's basket,
Queenie laid a single, perfect egg.

It was Caitlin who found the egg that morning.
And the next morning. And the next.

Every morning Queenie made her journey from the
farm to Caitlin's house and back,

leaving the gift of a small brown egg.

Only once did they spy on Queenie laying
her egg, and never again.

"It didn't seem right," said Mum. "It seemed…"
"Private," said Dad.

And so the weeks turned to months.

There were
changes in
Caitlin's house.

There was a new
baby in the family.

The story might have
ended right there …
but it didn't!

After the new baby came home,
Caitlin forgot to collect Queenie's eggs.

Bruno reclaimed his basket

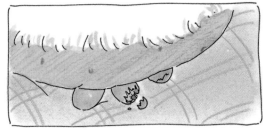

and Queenie never returned.

Bruno hatched the eggs …

CHICKS!

"Those chicks need their mother," said Mum.
So they all went back to the farm.

"There's Queenie!"
said Caitlin.

Caitlin's mum and dad and the new baby
came home with bread and milk and cheese.
And guess what Caitlin brought home!

Bruno made room for yet
another addition to the family!
One day the chick will be full grown and
will see Caitlin's brother take his first steps.

But that's another story.

BOB GRAHAM

Bob Graham is one of Australia's finest author-illustrators.
Winner of the Kate Greenaway Medal, Smarties Book Prize and CBCA
Picture Book of the Year, his stories are renowned for celebrating the magic
of everydayness. Bob says, *"I'd like reading my books to be a little like opening
a family photo album, glimpsing small moments captured from daily lives."*

ISBN 978-1-4063-1649-0

ISBN 978-1-4063-1613-1

ISBN 978-1-4063-1647-6

ISBN 978-1-4063-1640-7

ISBN 978-1-4063-1648-3

ISBN 978-1-4063-1650-6

ISBN 978-0-7445-9827-8

WINNER OF THE CBCA PICTURE BOOK
OF THE YEAR AWARD (2002)

ISBN 978-1-4063-0851-8

WINNER OF THE
KATE GREENAWAY MEDAL (2002)

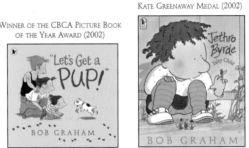

ISBN 978-1-84428-482-5

ISBN 978-1-4063-0132-8

ISBN 978-1-4063-0686-6

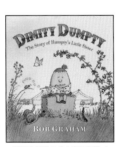

ISBN 978-1-84428-067-4

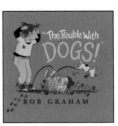

ISBN 978-1-4063-0338-4

ISBN 978-1-4063-0716-0

ISBN 978-1-4063-1492-2

Available from all good bookstores

www.walkerbooks.co.uk
www.walkerbooks.com.au